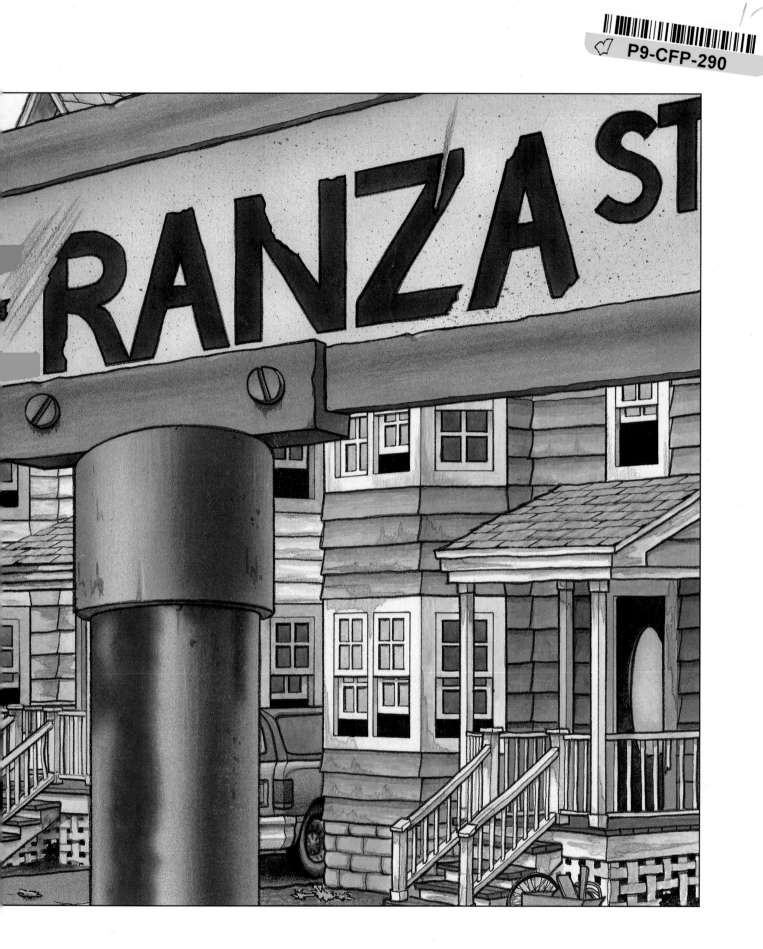

A GARDEN OF DREAMS is dedicated to children and adults
willing to take risks to make their dreams come true.
Richard M. Wainwright

Dedicated to my mother Caroline and father Len –
and again, with love, to my husband John.
Carolyn S. Dvorsack

FAMILY LIFE
PUBLISHING

Published by Family Life Publishing
Dennis, Massachusetts 02638

Printed in Singapore by Tien Wah Press
Published in the United States of America 1994

Library of Congress Cataloging in Publication Data

Wainwright, Richard M.
Garden of Dreams / written by Richard M. Wainwright:
illustrated by Carolyn Sansone Dvorsack,— 1st ed.

Summary:
The inhabitants of Esperanza Street, from many different cultural backgrounds, come together to
fulfill Anthony's dream of beautifying the neighborhood with a garden.

ISBN 0-9619566-6-6
[1. Gardens--Fiction. 2. City and town life--Fiction.]
I. Dvorsack, Carolyn Sansone, 1965- ill. Title.
PZ7. W1317Gar 1994
[Fic]--dc20 93-17974 CIP AC

Garden
of Dreams

Written by Richard M. Wainwright
Illustrated by Carolyn Sansone Dvorsack

To _Kendra_

Believe in your dreams,
you can make them come true.

Best Wishes,

Richard M. Wainwright

From _Grandma with love!_

*Best wishes —
your friend,
Richard M. Wainwright
1996*

*Happy Birthday
July 9th!*

Chapter

1 The people who lived on Esperanza Street frequently laughed at the name. Esperanza means "hope" in Spanish, and for many of the people who lived on the street, some days hope was all they could afford. The families had come from many different countries seeking a new and better life in the United States. Usually they arrived with little money and felt fortunate to be able to rent a small apartment on the edges of the city.

Esperanza Street was one of the oldest and, some said, shabbiest in the city. The houses were tired and worn—all cried out for a new coat of paint. Screen doors were tattered or bent; most wouldn't shut properly and swung back and forth in a strong breeze, slamming against the walls of the houses. A few broken windows, patched with pieces of cardboard, testified to the scarcity of dollars needed to repair them.

In front of each house was a small rectangular patch of dirt, bare except for an occasional weed that managed to survive until trampled to death by dogs, bikes or people. Paper bags, bottles, styrofoam cups and plates from fast food restaurants lay beside the weeds until kicked or blown to another spot down the street. Outside of the homes, it appeared there wasn't much hope on Esperanza Street.

Anthony slowly raised the torn window shade in his room where he slept with his younger brother, Michael. Between their beds on an old oak table stood a twenty gallon aquarium in which Mozart and Tchaikovksy, two whiskered Asian catfish, lazily circled the sides of the tank looking for food. Anthony's parents loved classical music and even Anthony liked some of it as much as his pop favorites. Thoughtfully, he looked down upon the street in front of their house. From his window he could easily see the sign on the corner: Esperanza Street.

Leaning on his elbows, daydreaming, he shifted his gaze to the small patch of ground below. "I wonder," he thought aloud. "Would it be possible? Maybe. I'll talk to Mr. Cocozza today."

After school, Anthony went to Mr. Cocozza's science room. Green plants filled window shelves. Glass tanks containing small animals and fish lined the walls. Mr. Cocozza was a big man and was called the "gentle giant" by students and teachers alike. He had played football in college and now coached the school's team. He greeted Anthony with a big smile. "Hi, Anthony," he said. "What's happening? Sit down."

Mr. Cocozza listened intently to Anthony's words. When Anthony had finished describing what he wanted to do, the big man smiled and nodded. "It's a great idea! A rock and flower garden in the city." Then his face grew serious. "Anthony," he continued, "having a garden is like caring for a family. It will take time, work, some money, and lots of tender loving care. And don't forget there may be disappointments too. Are you sure that you want to do this?"

"Yes," Anthony replied. "I have savings and I want to use it to start my garden."

Mr. Cocozza smiled and spoke. "All right, I have some extra tools you can use." For the next hour, Anthony and Mr. Cocozza worked together making lists and outlining the project step by step. Saturday morning they would begin.

Anthony could hardly wait for Mr. Cocozza to arrive. He had told his parents of his plans. Although they thought a garden wouldn't survive long on the street, they encouraged Anthony to try. Just before 9:00 A.M., Mr. Cocozza's blue pick-up truck came to a stop in front of Anthony's house. Anthony dashed down the stairs to greet him. In the back of the truck was a load of dirt, peat moss, a few large boulders, shovels and rakes. "First we dig for buried treasure," Mr. Cocozza said laughing. They began to turn over the soil. Broken bottles, small and medium-sized stones, brick and pieces of rotting wood appeared with every shovelful. "Look here," said Anthony, as he picked up a dirty but intact dark-bluish bottle.

"Save that one," said Mr. Cocozza. "It looks pretty old."

It was hard work digging into and turning over the packed ground which probably had not been disturbed for over seventy years. As Anthony and his teacher dug, a few people who lived on the street stopped to watch them. Curious, they speculated on the reason for the hard work of the two. As they dug, the trash pile grew. Someone suggested that maybe they really were looking for buried treasure. Everyone laughed at this idea, and Mr. Cocozza looked over at Anthony and winked.

As the crowd increased, a thin old man joined them. People drew back making a path for him. Demetrious Constantine Kerriokas slowly moved to the front. "Mr. K" was loved by all who lived on Esperanza Street. He knew each adult and child by first and last name and even the cats and dogs that somehow survived the constant traffic of a city street. From a block away, a neighbor would recognize Esperanza Street's oldest inhabitant. Mr. Kerriokas had silver hair and a matching, neatly trimmed mustache. He always wore a spotless white shirt, navy tie and a clean but worn, old-fashioned dark blue suit. His clothes reminded adults of years gone by. His bright black eyes, infectious smile and cheery greetings encouraged everyone to remember to be thankful for their personal blessings. He was a living symbol of hope. Mr. Kerriokas would stroll daily up and down the street, stopping to chat with anyone passing by. People always seemed to feel better after they had talked with Mr. K.

Mr. K knew immediately what Anthony had in mind, and his heart smiled, thinking back over sixty years to his garden in Greece. He remembered that the soil in the mountains there hadn't been very good either. In Greece there hadn't been trash, but there had been lots and lots of rocks. Although he loved his garden and had worked very hard, even in good years the land barely produced enough to feed his family.

After three bad harvests in a row, he and his family were desperate, so Demetrious Constantine Kerriokas prayed. Then, with his family's meager savings, the Kerriokas family emigrated to the United States. It had not been easy when they arrived. None of his family spoke a word of English, and finding work was a daily challenge for Mr. K. Like most immigrants, with a little help Demetrious soon learned the ropes of making a living in the U.S., and his family not only survived but also came to love their new country. His three children went to school, studied hard and received a fine education. After graduation they were offered good jobs. Sadly for Mr. K and his wife Andrea, those jobs took their children away from the city. His children married and now had families of their own. Mrs. Kerriokas lived long enough to see ten grandchildren born. Mr. K now lived alone; alone until his children, grandchildren, and his three great-grandchildren came to visit. For years, every member of his family tried to convince Mr. K to move out of the city and live in the country with a son or daughter, but he always shook his head. Esperanza Street was his home.

"Gotcha!" shouted Mr. Cocozza, as the old tire that had been deeply buried broke free and was added to the trash pile. "I think that's the lot," he called to Anthony, who was picking up a few small stones.

Mr. Cocozza asked the crowd to make way so he could back the truck closer. When it was in position, he and Anthony climbed up and began shoveling the loam out of the truck. They had planned a terraced rock garden for flowers—annuals and perennials. It took half an hour to empty the truck. Then they opened bags of peat moss and fertilizer. With rakes and shovels, Anthony and Mr. Cocozza worked hard, mixing loam, peat and fertilizer before spreading it over the garden. They made several distinct terraces, building the garden higher and higher as they got closer to the house. Mr. Cocozza and Anthony returned to the truck for the three large boulders. Several men and Anthony's friends offered to help move the large stones. Carefully, the gang of men and boys placed the large boulders one by one in the garden. A beautiful granite boulder which contained some sparkling quartz was placed at the highest point.

Anthony looked down at the crowd and caught Mr. Kerriokas's eye. "This stone," he announced with a big smile, "will be our Mt. Olympus." Mr. K beamed and everyone applauded and whistled approval.

Finally, Anthony and Mr. Cocozza stood back, joining the people who had remained to watch. "What do you think of the design?" Mr. Cocozza asked the people nearby. "Very nice." "Professional." "Terrific," they replied. Anthony moved beside Mr. Kerriokas. "What do you think, Mr. K?" Anthony asked. Mr. K put his hand on Anthony's shoulder. "I think it is just wonderful. Don't change a thing. It's ready for planting." Anthony smiled. He agreed. The initial hard work was done. Now the fun would begin, deciding where to put the marigold and zinnia seeds and then planting them.

As Mr. Cocozza and Anthony discussed the planting, the on-lookers slowly drifted away until only old Mr. Kerriokas remained. He loved the smell of the newly turned earth and he enjoyed watching Anthony and his teacher dig the shallow holes and carefully plant the seeds. Mr. Kerriokas's mind carried him back and forth from Esperanza Street to the dirt road that had bordered his garden in Greece. At this moment he was happier than he had been in years. He had never expected to see a garden on this street. Somehow, he thought, maybe he could help Anthony.

Anthony spent Sunday planting snapdragons and watering the garden, especially the two boxes of petunias Mr. Cocozza had purchased for him as a gift. He also decided on the names of the other two boulders: Mt. McKinley would be one and Mt. Everest would be the other. As he worked, neighbors and friends stopped by to say hello and to wish him luck. Mr. Kerriokas often appeared, but after exchanging greetings with Anthony, contented himself with standing quietly and watching him care for his garden.

Monday morning Anthony finished his breakfast more quickly than usual to spend a few minutes watering his garden. Holding the nozzle, he slowly directed the fine spray from side to side giving the garden a good soaking.

"Hi Anthony," David called as he approached. "I'd like to put in an order for a bunch of carnations for my mother's birthday." David was Anthony's best friend. They always walked to school together.

Anthony laughed, "I'm happy to take your order but don't hold your breath until delivery. Everything looks fine today but as Mr. Cocozza said, 'A lot can happen between now and picking time.'"

David pointed to his watch. Anthony nodded and turned off the water, coiled the hose, put it on the holder and picked up his school bag; the boys knew they had to hustle.

Later in the day, before leaving school, Anthony had a chance to thank Mr. Cocozza again for his help. "Glad to do it," he replied. "You've got a real challenge, Anthony. A garden in the city won't be easy. Give it your best shot and keep me posted. Let me know if there is anything else I can do. Now I'm off to the football practice." Mr. Cocozza gave Anthony a pat on the back and headed down the corridor.

Anthony felt terrific. It was a gorgeous spring day. He had received a very good grade on a tough math test and was looking forward to a game of stickball when he got home. David was waiting at the exit door. He was also in a good mood as he too had aced the exam. Both boys took their school work seriously, often studying together late in the afternoon or in the early evening.

From the corner of Esperanza Street to Anthony's house was less than a hundred yards. Glancing toward his garden in the distance, he could only sense something was wrong. A few seconds later both boys were staring at Anthony's garden. Mini-mountains of dirt stood at the edge of several large holes that had been recently dug. The clumps of petunias Mr. Cocozza gave Anthony were unearthed, exposing their rapidly drying roots to the strong rays of the sun. Seeds lay scattered here and there on the surface. "Dogs!" Anthony angrily exclaimed, and David sadly nodded. "I had better change my clothes before trying to save the petunias and replanting the seeds. See you later, Dave." Before his friend could reply, Anthony dashed up the steps to his house.

A few minutes later when Anthony opened his front door, Mr. K was standing beside the garden. "Yasu, Anthony," said Mr. Kerriokas. (Yasu means 'hello' in Greek.) "I see you have had some unwelcome visitors. Dogs especially love newly turned earth to dig in. What you need is a 'filakas.'"

"Yasu, Mr. K," Anthony replied. "But, what is a 'filakas'?"

"A filakas, my young friend, means 'guardian' in Greek, or to be specific in this particular case, a garden watcher; and I would like to apply for the job. No payment required—only a bouquet of your flowers someday for my kitchen table." Mr. K smiled, waiting for Anthony's answer.

Anthony grinned and held out his hand. "You're hired, Mr. K. You are the official 'filakas' of my garden and I want you to be my horticultural advisor too. My parents told me that you had a garden in Greece and I know I will need lots of help if my garden is to amount to anything."

Anthony couldn't have made Mr. Kerriokas happier. "I'll do all I can," Mr. K replied. "My one hope is that the weather will be our friend: some sun, some rain, and not too much of either at once. Now you had better replant those petunias and seeds before the sun kills them. Give them another drink of water before you go in and don't worry. I'll be on duty bright and early."

Anthony smiled and waved good-bye as he stepped into his garden. He felt much better and was no longer angry at the dogs. He had a partner and new friend. His garden had produced its first blossom. Anthony knelt in the dirt and began the replanting. He thought of Mr. K and an idea came to his mind.

That evening after he finished his homework, Anthony made something special for Mr. Kerriokas and planned to give it to him when he returned from school tomorrow.

When Anthony opened his front door the next morning he was the first to be surprised. There was Mr. K sitting in a beach chair on the sidewalk beside the garden reading the morning newspaper. "Good morning, Mr. Kerriokas," Anthony greeted his friend.

"Kalimara," Mr. K answered, smiling.

Anthony paused by Mr. Kerriokas and opened one of his school books. Between the pages was the gift he had made. It was a gold badge with the words OFFICIAL FILAKAS neatly printed in black in the center. Anthony handed it to Mr. Kerriokas and smiled.

Mr. Kerriokas grinned from ear to ear. "That's terrific, Anthony. I will be proud to wear it. Thanks very much. Here comes your friend, David. Study hard and I will see you after school."

Each day before Anthony left for school, Mr. Kerriokas would be at his post beside the garden. As the sun rose higher, Mr. K would attach a red and white umbrella to his chair. Besides the newspaper, he would read magazines, and he always brought one book. Some days Mr. Kerriokas did not get much time to read. An occasional dog would be admonished to stay out of the garden, but mostly it was neighbors who interrupted him. Of course, Mr. Kerriokas loved to chat with everyone. He learned how their families were doing and talked about Anthony's garden and the flowers they hoped to grow. In the afternoon when Anthony returned and carefully weeded and watered the garden, he and Mr. Kerriokas would talk about gardening in particular and everything in general including the latest news of Esperanza Street.

The weather was unusually warm for spring. Two weeks after Anthony and Mr. Cocozza planted the garden, Mr. Kerriokas and Anthony could see that most of the seeds had germinated. Little green shoots were everywhere. Anthony had to be especially careful now when he stepped into the garden to weed and tend the young plants. Soon they were an inch high. "They're just beginning to develop roots," Mr. Kerriokas commented.

Sometimes Anthony couldn't tell the difference between a weed and a tiny plant, but Mr. Kerriokas always seemed to know. Looking up at the sky one late afternoon, Mr. Kerriokas spoke. "Anthony, I think we can skip the watering today. Unless I miss my guess, those gray clouds rolling in are going to give us a good soaking. I'll see you tomorrow."

"Good night, Mr. Kerriokas," Anthony replied. He didn't notice the worried look on Mr. K's face as he turned and folded up his chair before heading home. The old man knew the freshening breeze and the quickly forming thunderheads would indeed bring a heavy rainstorm.

As the crash of another bolt of lightning lit up the sky, Anthony stared out his bedroom window. Sheets of pelting rain hammered the glass. Even Mozart and Tchaikovsky pressed together in a far corner of their fish tank, seeming to be very much aware of the ferocious storm raging outside. Only Anthony's younger brother Michael remained blissfully asleep. Hours went by before the thunder and lightning lessened. Finally Anthony went back to bed. The heavy tapping of steady rain continued, lulling Anthony into a worried sleep.

The bright morning sun streamed in the window, slowly moving higher until it beamed on Anthony's face. He had slept later than usual, even for a Saturday. Then Anthony remembered the night's violent storm. He got up quickly and went over to the window. What he saw brought tears to his eyes. Anthony slowly shook his head. "All that work, time and money gone, wasted and nothing left."

Anthony stared at what had been his garden. The tiny seedlings were gone, probably dying somewhere in the pile of dirt which had been washed onto the sidewalk and even into the street. At least half of the loam of the garden had been carried away. Anthony covered his eyes with his hands. He was beaten. Nature was an enemy, not a friend. He felt crushed, angry and tired from his interrupted hours of sleep. It was a sad Saturday morning. He pulled down the shade and went back to bed and closed his eyes.

Anthony tossed and turned as he dreamed a crazy dream. Along with his garden tools, he and Mr. Kerriokas were being propelled down

Esperanza Street by a sea of rainwater. Anthony almost laughed in the dream as Mr. Kerriokas was sitting high and dry in his beach chair which magically didn't sink, but majestically floated on top of the swirling waters. Mr. K was talking about the importance of water for gardens as if nothing was happening, while Anthony desperately clung to Mr. Kerriokas's chair with one hand and to the handle of a rake with the other. Strange voices, weak at first and then becoming louder, came from the houses as Anthony and Mr. K were being swept down the street by the huge wave.

Anthony slowly opened his eyes. "What a crazy dream," he thought, and then he remembered the storm and what had happened to his garden. He could still hear voices, but now he was definitely awake. He returned to his front window and heard Mr. K's unmistakable voice.

"Very good, Mrs. Chu; right over there will be fine. That's a good spot, Mrs. Salame, thank you. Ah, Mrs. Robinski, you've come to help too. Wonderful. Tania, is that your new beach pail you are using? Thank you, Mohammed, we can use another rake. Mrs. Becerra, you have the eye of a gardener. Hi Tom and Mrs. Greene. Ah, another shovel, just what we need. Oh, here's the Coe family. Good morning, and welcome!"

Anthony raised the window shade. He couldn't believe his eyes. Below him was a mass of people. Standing on top of Mt. McKinley was Mr. Kerriokas like a symphony conductor directing the crowd of people scooping up the mud from the sidewalk and street using pots, pans, pails, rakes and shovels, and depositing it as directed back onto the garden. Even some of the youngest children who lived on the street had large spoons and were trying to help.

For a few moments, Anthony could only stare. He thought of the ant colony display in Mr. Cocozza's room and had to laugh. It seemed that

Mr. K had not given up on the garden. Anthony shook his head and smiled as he rushed to get dressed and hurried to join Mr. Kerriokas's mud-moving orchestra. Many willing hands labored together to recapture as much of the loam as possible for Anthony's garden. Mrs. Tomasian swept up the last pile of dirt from the street and carried it toward Mt. Olympus. Anthony's neighbors, who had worked so hard, applauded. Before returning to their homes many said a few words of encouragement to Anthony. Some simply gave him the "thumbs-up" sign, or waved as they left. Finally, only Mr. Kerriokas remained. He opened up his beach chair and sat down. Anthony, covered with mud and still holding his shovel, went and stood in front of him.

Mr. K looked up at Anthony and asked, "Well, my young friend, do we begin again?"

Anthony hesitated for only a moment, and with a resigned smile and a firm voice replied, "Yes, Mr. K, we begin again."

Anthony turned back to the pile of muddy loam and began to rake and reshape his garden. Mr. Kerriokas watched proudly and occasionally made encouraging suggestions. He knew from experience how tough it was to lose everything and start over.

It wasn't long before Anthony's mother arrived with a plate of sandwiches and milk for her son and Mr. Kerriokas. Like many days which follow a storm, there wasn't a cloud in the sky. The air smelled especially fresh and clean and a bright sun soon forced Anthony to take off his shirt. By the time late afternoon shadows crossed the street, Anthony had re-designed and prepared his garden for another planting.

"Well, Mr. K," said Anthony, leaning on his rake, "I guess we're ready to plant. Now all I need to do is earn some money for seeds and fertilizer."

Mr. Kerriokas nodded seriously and then a hint of a smile spread across his face. "Keep the faith, Anthony," he replied. "Tomorrow is another day. There is always hope, and life is full of surprises."

Chapter 3

It had been a few days since the rainstorm and the flash flooding on Esperanza Street. Anthony and his family finished eating their breakfast together, and then, as was their custom, everyone pitched in to do the dishes. Saturday morning's room cleaning was Anthony's next responsibility along with the feeding of Mozart and Tchaikovsky. When he was finished, Anthony went downstairs to the street, and walked around what had been his garden. Thanks to his neighbors, most of the loam had been saved, but the bare dirt certainly didn't look anything like a garden. With the exception of the large stones, it now looked even more barren than the other dirt fronts on the street which at least had produced a few green weeds. Anthony stared sadly at his garden. He remembered telling Mr. Kerriokas that he would try again, but his piggy bank and wallet were empty and the prospect of finding a job quickly to earn enough money wasn't good.

The sun was almost directly overhead, and Anthony remembered he had at least three hours of homework before nightfall. He also knew that simply staring at the garden wasn't accomplishing anything. With a shrug and final glance, Anthony went inside to study. The homework wasn't easy, but Anthony got good grades because he was able to concentrate and focus all his energy on one assignment at a time. Time flew. Only when his mom brought him some milk and a sandwich did he realize that it was late in the afternoon. Sometime later, Anthony was vaguely aware of a car coming to a stop near the front of his house. This wasn't unusual, as often neighbors' friends parked in front of their house. His mind returned to his homework, but only for a few minutes. The doorbell rang.

"Anthony!" his mother called. "Someone would like to speak with you."

"Someone?" Anthony wondered. Mom always mentioned the boy's or girl's name. He quickly tied his sneakers and hurried down the stairs.

"Someone" turned out to be ten adults and lots of children. The little ones surrounded Mr. Kerriokas. Anthony stopped. He could see over the heads of everyone, and there were even more people outside.

Little Tania, dressed in her nicest dress, came forward with a box tied with a blue ribbon. Her eyes were huge and shining. She was smiling. Tania spoke only a few words. "Anthony," she began, "we want to see beautiful flowers on our street." Without another word she handed the box to Anthony. People applauded, smiled, laughed and quietly waited.

"Open the box, Anthony!" Mr. K whispered.

Anthony untied the ribbon and raised the cover. Inside the box were colorful packages of flower seeds and some bulbs. Anthony didn't know what to say. He knew everyone must have contributed. Picking up one package so all could see, he spoke in a quiet but determined voice. "Monday we plant again. Thank you all very much." There was more clapping and almost as one, Anthony's neighbors and friends turned to go.

Mr. Kerriokas smiled, slowly rose and paused. Anthony could see the twinkle in his eyes as he began to speak. "Yesterday, my son drove in from the country with loam, petunias, and chicken manure. Flowers love it! See you later." Anthony chuckled and gave Mr. K a gentle pat on the back as the old man followed the throng down the steps.

Monday after school, Anthony wasn't surprised to find Mr. K sitting in his sidewalk chair beside six large boxes. "Be back in five," Anthony called as he dashed into the house to change his clothes. Minutes later he began spreading the loam and chicken manure. By late Friday afternoon, with Mr. K's advice, Anthony thought he had planted all the seeds, bulbs and plants, but he was wrong. Mr. Kerriokas opened his hand which held three large seeds. "Anthony, these seeds were sent to me from an old friend in Greece. Would you mind trying to grow a squash in your flower garden?"

Anthony took the seeds from Mr. K's hand and replied, "Our garden will have the best squash this side of the Acropolis." Mr. Kerriokas laughed as Anthony planted the seeds behind Mt. Olympus.

A few days later, school was out for the summer. The daily sun was strong. Mr. K and Anthony knew their garden needed water almost every day, and water it got. It wasn't long before green stalks pushed their way through the ground and were followed almost overnight by leaves. Each new bud on a leaf was spotted by Anthony and Mr. K, and soon the first flowers—beautiful marigolds, zinnias, snapdragons, tulips and of course, petunias—blossomed. Neighbors with their children came by at least once each day to stand and admire the flowers which seemed to be exploding like a Fourth of July fireworks display. Not one flower was touched until Tania came by. Anthony stopped his weeding, and with a wink toward Mr. K, picked a bright gold marigold and handed it to Tania. His reward was a big hug before Tania scampered off to show her mother.

Anthony carefully stepped into his garden to do a little weeding as Mr. Kerriokas changed the position of his chair. "What a gorgeous day, Anthony," Mr. Kerriokas began; "blue sky, the smell of flowers," and then Mr. K paused, "the crack of the stickball bat."

Anthony heard the "crack" too, followed by boys cheering, and then the "kerplunk" of the tennis ball landing smack in the middle of the garden. Anthony frowned as he slowly moved to retrieve it, but he wasn't fast enough for his friend David, who leapt into the garden after the ball.

"Watch out for my flowers! Get out!!!" yelled Anthony as he pushed David as hard as he could. Off balance, David staggered backward squashing one of Anthony's clumps of petunias. Now, he too mad. He forgot about the ball as Anthony grabbed him and both boys fell to the ground. Wrestling, the two friends crushed more and more flowers. Only seconds went by before two young men jumped into the garden and separated the fighting boys. Anthony and David, best of friends minutes before, glared at each other. The older boys told Anthony they would move the stickball game further down the street and then they turned, taking David with them.

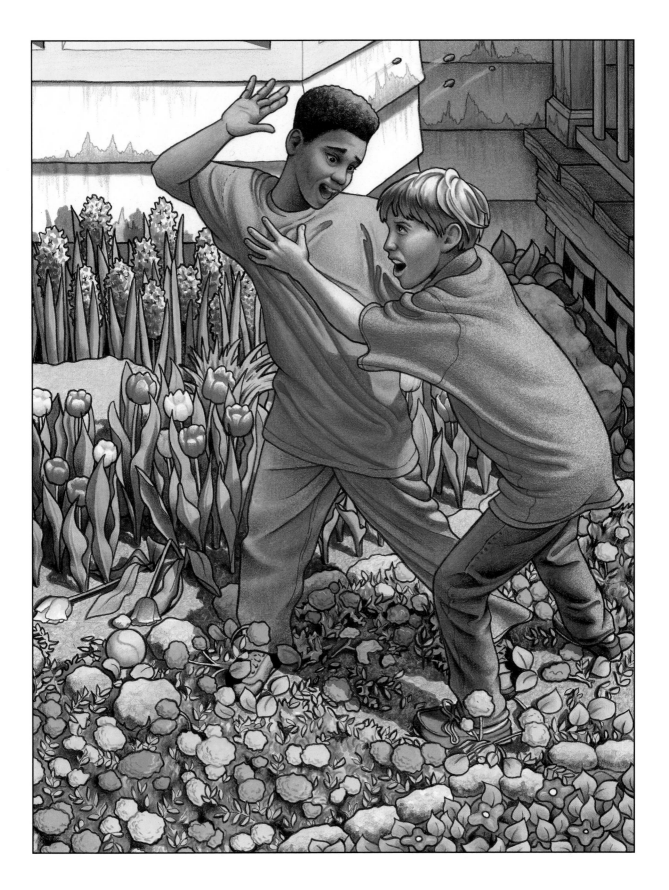

Anthony sat down on the curb and stared at his trampled garden. "Another disaster! Was the garden worth it?" His clothes were filthy and his shirt pocket was torn. His mother would be mad and he thought many of his plants would die. Sadly, he shook his head. "Maybe having a garden in the city was a stupid idea."

"Anthony," Mr. Kerriokas called, "come over here, please, and sit down next to me." Anthony had completely forgotten about his old friend and looked up into his worried face. "This garden means a lot to you, Anthony," Mr. Kerriokas continued. "It means a lot to me, too. I can understand how you felt when David jumped into it. When I was your age, I probably would have reacted the same way you did, but you didn't really need to. Strong plants, like most people, are very resilient. That means even when they have been knocked down or badly bruised, with a little love and care they will bounce back and be just fine. You and I both love flowers. Every day they remind us of all of nature's miracles, but believe me, people are much more important than flowers. Good friends are not easily replaced. Friendships are truly precious and can be strong, yet at the same time fragile. With care and thoughtfulness friendships will last longer and provide more happiness than the most beautiful flower we can grow. Do you understand what I am trying to tell you?"

Anthony's head dropped. He didn't answer right away. "Yes, Mr. Kerriokas," Anthony replied softly, "I do understand. I was wrong to get so angry. I'll go over to David's house after supper and tell him I'm sorry."

"Good!" said Mr. Kerriokas, smiling and patting Anthony on the back. "Now, get back into your garden, pack a little extra dirt around those plants that have been damaged, and give everyone a good drink of water. I guarantee in two days our green friends will be standing tall again."

Anthony returned Mr. K's grin, got up and stepped back into his garden. As he bent down to work he thought of Mr. Kerriokas' advice. He knew he would remember it as long as he lived.

Anthony was unusually quiet during supper, thinking about what he would say to David. As he excused himself from the table the doorbell rang. "I'll see who it is," Anthony said, starting for the door.

Pulling open the door, Anthony stared in surprise. David and his father stood before him. "Can we come in?" David asked.

" Sure, please, I ... I was just leaving to come over to see you. Honest! I wanted to apologize for losing my temper and fighting with you this afternoon. Mr. Kerriokas made me realize that our friendship is much more important than my garden."

David smiled and his father chuckled. "I came to tell you it was my fault," David began. " I should have watched where I was going. Everyone knows how hard you have worked to create your garden. Your neighbors

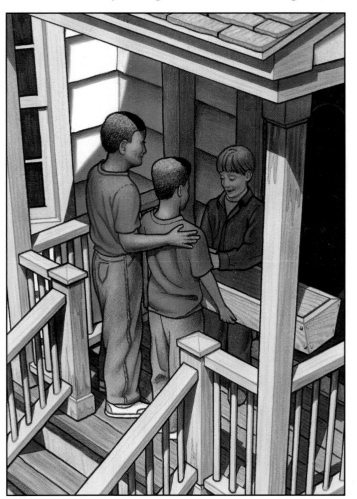

are proud of you and really appreciate being able to watch your flowers grow and blossom. You have given every person who lives on Esperanza Street something to look forward to each day. I'm sorry we fought, too. My dad is a carpenter and he helped me make this flower box for your house. If you like it, I'll be glad to help you paint it tomorrow."

"Thanks. Thanks a lot, David," Anthony replied, thrusting out his arm and shaking David's hand. Then he shook David's father's hand, as he accepted the flower box.

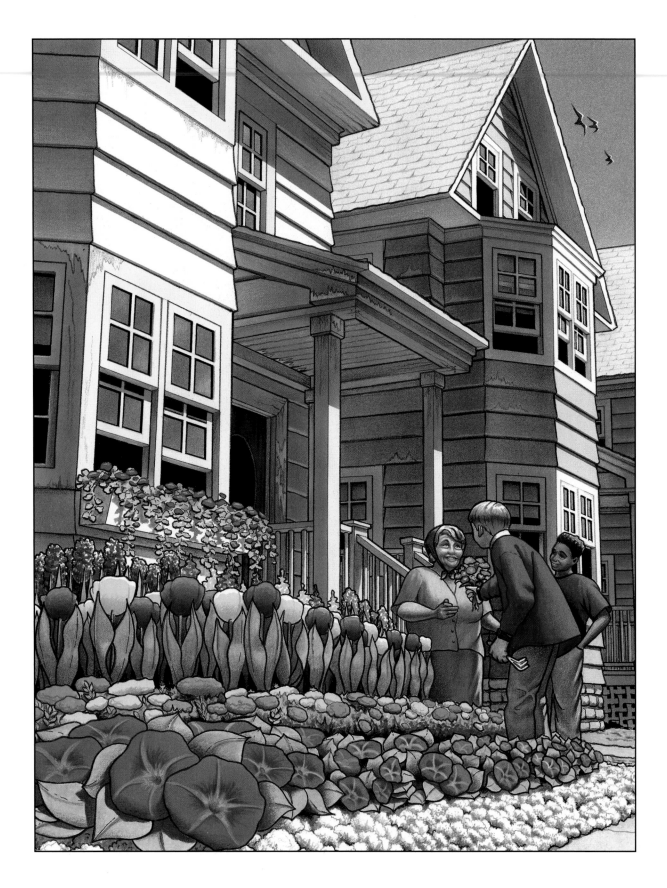

Chapter

The following morning David and Anthony painted the flower box white and, while they waited for it to dry, Anthony pointed out some new flowers that were about to blossom. Then Mr. K showed up and told David all about the special Greek squash that was growing behind Mt. Olympus.

The boys left for a quick game of stickball, returning to meet David's father, who had promised to put up the brackets for the flower box during his lunch hour. It didn't take them long to level the brackets and screw them tightly to the wall. Anthony's mom appeared, carrying four large ivy geraniums, and the boys immediately planted them in the flower box before lifting it onto its supports. Everyone then stepped back to admire the colorful bouquet under the window.

The next day, Mrs. Rabinski was the first to notice the flower box. Anthony was doing a little weeding. "Your flowers are just beautiful," she began, "and your new flower box is lovely. Maybe someday I could have one built for my house, but they are so expensive." Anthony smiled, stopped weeding and talked with Mrs. Rabinski for a few minutes, and then picked a few flowers for her. She thanked Anthony and started home thinking how lovely the fresh flowers would look on her dining-room table.

During the next few days, it seemed to Anthony and David that as soon as they stepped outside or began working in the garden, one or more of the ladies who lived on Esperanza Street would stop by and echo Mrs. Rabinski's sentiments. Everyone wished they too could look outside and see flowers growing in their own window box. Even Anthony's and David's friends would drop by and tell them how much the garden meant to their parents and that the new window box was really nice.

Finally, David winked at Anthony and commented, "How many hints does that make, Anthony?"

"According to my count, we have now heard from everyone except your folks and Mr. K," Anthony laughed. "If we count your house and Mr. K's, we would need twenty-two flower boxes."

Anthony's face became serious as he continued, "You know, David, if my neighbors hadn't scooped up the loam after the storm and bought those seeds and new plants, my garden would be just another weed patch today, with paper cup blossoms. Wouldn't it be great if we could give every house on the street a painted window box filled with flowers?"

"Hold on, my man," David cut in. "Our families together couldn't afford the wood and paint for twenty-two window boxes, not to mention filling them with flowers. You're talking big bucks. Our families are just like everybody else on this street. Putting food on the table, paying the rent and buying clothes are a tough job for our parents. You'll have to write Santa for this one."

"I know, I know," Anthony commented. "But I've got a long shot idea. I'm going to call Mr. Cocozza and see if he will come by tomorrow. Come on over at ten and hear what he has to say."

"Say, about what?" David asked. Anthony just winked and smiled.

When Anthony called Mr. Cocozza later, his teacher's first words were, "Anthony, I was just about to call you. I have some information that might be of interest to you. See you at ten."

The next morning, David came by a few minutes early. He found Anthony sitting in the living room. In front of him was a beautiful cobalt-blue bottle with a bust of George Washington etched on it, and the words LOCKPORT GLASS WORKS raised in a horseshoe framed the face. As Mr. Cocozza entered the room he greeted the boys and sat down. He told Anthony how great his garden oasis looked as he came down the street.

"Welcome, Mr. Cocozza," Anthony began, "thanks for coming by. Do you remember the dirty old bottle we dug up the day we started the garden? I cleaned it up. What do you think? Could it possibly be valuable?"

Mr. Cocozza carefully picked up the lovely bottle. "You just may be right, Anthony," he replied, "and if you are, this bottle will make what I am going to tell you possible. But first, tell me what you have in mind."

Anthony told Mr. Cocozza about how his neighbors had provided the second chance for him to have a garden. He described their work in the mud and how they had all chipped in to buy more seeds and plants. He asked David to tell "Mr. C" about their fight and the resulting flower box David's father had built, and how much everyone on the street wanted a window box of his own. He even mentioned that people seemed to care more for their street and that there wasn't as much trash lying around.

"My hope, Mr. Cocozza," Anthony continued, "is that maybe this old bottle is worth enough money to build and paint window boxes for every house on Esperanza Street and fill them with flowers. Our fathers think that would take close to five hundred dollars, and that's a lot of money."

Mr. Cocozza rubbed his chin as he examined the beautiful blue bottle. "One of my colleagues, Dayton Nelson, and his wife Polly, spend a lot of weekends digging in the country looking for old bottles. They have a wonderful collection and I bet they could tell us how much this bottle is worth. I'll show it to them tomorrow, but before I go, I wanted you and David to know of a 4-H Exhibition and Country Fair which is scheduled for the end of August. They have all sorts of demonstrations, exhibits and animals. You could even enter Mr. Kerriokas's squash in one of the horticultural competitions. It's a four day event, lots of fun, and a great way to meet young people from all over the United States. The only problem is that it would cost you two hundred dollars for food, tickets, and a motel room. I would be happy to take you but I know it's a lot of money.

"It sounds wonderful," Anthony commented, "but right now my folks don't have any extra money, and what I am able to earn has to go to pay for clothes and some of the water bill which is higher because of our garden."

David smiled. "It sounds great to me, too, Mr. Cocozza, but we are in the same boat as Anthony's folks. Times are tough for us."

Mr. Cocozza nodded and carefully picked up the old bottle as he rose to leave. "It's a long shot, but maybe this bottle will grant both your wishes. Keep your fingers crossed. I'll let you know what the Nelsons say."

The summer routine continued. David and Anthony would meet by the garden early to water and weed. Of course, Mr. Kerriokas was always there waiting, settled in his beach chair reading a newspaper and ready to raise his umbrella as the sun turned hot. After chatting with Mr. K about the garden and doing what was needed, the boys would go off looking for work around the neighborhood to try to earn some money. If there wasn't any work, there was usually a stickball or basketball game at the park. On real hot days, a fire hydrant would be turned on in the afternoon so everyone could cool off.

Late afternoon was "picking time," and the boys would make up a bouquet for one of their neighbors and then deliver it. All the families that lived on the street would make a point of walking by Anthony's garden at least once a day to enjoy the rainbow of flowers and point out buds just about to open.

Several weeks went by and Anthony had almost given up hope that his bottle would bring good news. One night as he and his family were watching T.V., the phone rang. "Hi, Anthony, how are you?" the caller began. It was Mr. Cocozza. "I've got some good and not-so-good news for you. According to the Nelsons, your bottle is a rare flask over one hundred years old. It would be worth five hundred dollars to a collector; maybe even a little more since it is in perfect condition. They would be happy to buy it from you for that price. What do you think, Anthony?"

"That's great!" Anthony replied. "Just terrific! What's the not-so-good news?"

"Well," Mr. Cocozza continued, "the money will allow you and David either to build your window boxes or to join me on that trip up north to the Country Fair. You have a tough choice to make."

Anthony paused for just a moment before answering. "Mr. Cocozza, David and I would love to go with you and I know it would be a fantastic experience for us. The trip would make two people very happy, but with the five hundred dollars, David and I can make a lot more people happy here on Esperanza Street."

"Anthony," Mr. Cocozza said, "I understand. It's a wonderful and generous decision. You're a special young man. I will bring the money to your house tomorrow evening. Take care."

The next morning Anthony excitedly told David and Mr. K the good news. He didn't even mention the Country Fair. David's father returned home for lunch and he and the boys sat at the kitchen table writing out a list of supplies they would need to build, paint, and fill with flowers twenty-two window boxes.

"Gentlemen," David's father said, "this is a great project, but I think you are going to need some help. Why not ask your friends? The Svendsen brothers are good workers and I think David's older sister, Julienne, would be glad to help. As you know she can really handle a paint brush."

Anthony and David thought it was a good idea, and left looking for volunteers. A little to their surprise, every friend they asked on Esperanza Street wanted to help.

The boys agreed that the building of the window boxes would begin the following afternoon. Mr. Cocozza, Anthony and David would pick up the lumber, nails, paint and flowers in the morning. Later, everyone would meet in front of Anthony's house, and David's father would bring the hammers and saws.

Chapter

By 2:00 P.M. eighteen boys and girls were ready to begin. It didn't take long for David's father to set up the saw horses and divide the young people into teams. He showed the "builders" how to measure and cut the lumber. Anthony and David captained the "assemblers" who carefully screwed the pieces of wood together to make the window boxes and then bored drain holes in the bottom.

Julienne was in charge of the "painters" who had covered the sidewalk with old newspapers and were waiting for the first finished window box. With David's father's help, it wasn't long before the boys proudly handed Julienne the first completed window box.

The neighborhood echoed with the sounds of accomplishment as saws sang, hammers pounded, and paint brushes swished along with shouts and chatter from the boys and girls. Blending in was the week's Top 40 providing the beat from Julienne's large portable radio. The word of the project had spread like wildfire, and most of the neighbors turned out to watch the window box factory in action. It was a wonderful spectacle. It wasn't long before some of the older folks arrived with cookies, pieces of cake, and gallons of lemonade. David's father, while munching on a brownie, kept moving from group to group answering questions and encouraging slow, accurate work. "We want these window boxes to last for many, many years," he told everyone.

As soon as a window box was completed, it was passed on to Julienne's painting team for its prime coat of white. The hours flew by. When the "sawers" had finished their work, they helped Anthony and David until the final window box was built. A cheer went up, but David's father shouted, "No time to rest yet, guys and girls. Follow me." He led Anthony, David, and the boys and girls who had finished, toward the houses

at the far end of Esperanza Street. David and Anthony carried a box of metal brackets.

Anthony rang the front doorbell. Mrs. Herrera, who had heard of the project, was anxiously waiting, and she rushed to the door. She was patient as Anthony and David explained their idea and finally asked if she would like to have a window box under her front window.

As soon as Anthony paused, Mrs. Herrera reached out and kissed both boys and even surprised David's father with a hug. "Of course, I would love a window box," she stammered, "and I promise I will take good care of my flowers. Anthony, your garden is the nicest thing that has ever happened on Esperanza Street, and I've been here over twenty-two years." Mrs. Herrera paused for breath. A very embarrassed Anthony thanked her, and said they were going to put up the brackets now and would return tomorrow with the window box.

By now David's father was showing the workers how to measure and install the brackets. Anthony and David did the first one together. After the brackets were installed to David's father's satisfaction, the group of young people divided into "bracket installation teams," and left to visit the rest of the houses on Esperanza Street. By the time the street lights came on, every house had a set of brackets under its front windows.

They all returned to Anthony's house just as Julienne and her crew were finishing the second coat of paint on the window boxes. "Thanks to David's father and all my friends, we got a lot done today," Anthony thought. "Tomorrow will be a long day, too, but planting the geraniums will be fun."

Anthony thanked everyone as he and David's family gathered up the tools and Julienne picked up the old newspapers that were splattered with white paint. Before drifting off, many of Anthony's friends sat down on Anthony's front steps and talked about what they had accomplished. The smells of fresh paint, flowers and sawdust seemed to linger in the air. It was going to be a beautiful night in a nice part of the world.

Indeed, the next day was long and hot, and Anthony and David began their work soon after dawn. Mr. K, as usual, sat in his beach chair next to Anthony's garden, chatting and encouraging the boys as they worked. Loam and fertilizer were mixed before the geraniums were planted in the flower boxes. After watering the flowers, the boys loaded the now heavy window box onto Michael's little red wagon. Slowly they pulled it down the street to Mrs. Herrera, who again made a big fuss over the boys as they lifted the window box onto its brackets.

All day long the boys repeated the process of filling and delivering each window box. Everyone thanked them for their generosity and for all they had done to make Esperanza Street a nicer place to live. Of course each neighbor insisted they have something to eat and drink. After the third house the boys were full of milk, soda, sandwiches and cookies. Yet the people insisted they take something back home with them. First they shared the goodies with Mr. K, but he never ate much. It wasn't long before Anthony's and David's refrigerators were crammed full of food. Anthony's mother jokingly said she wouldn't have to shop for at least a month. Finally only

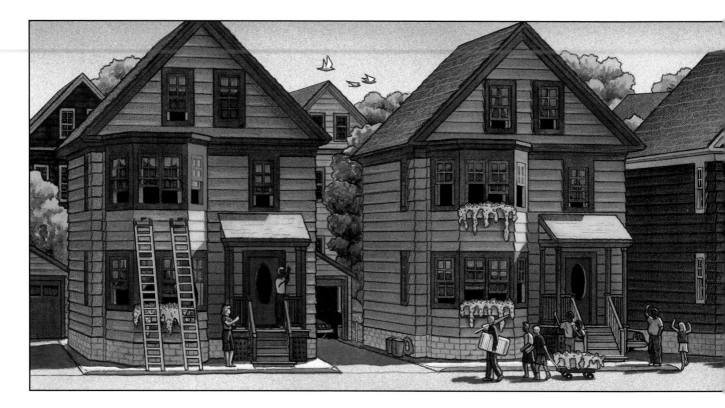

one window box remained, and it belonged to Mr. K.

"Sir Filakas," Anthony began with a big grin, "will you accompany us while we install your window box?"

Mr. Kerriokas smiled, slowly rose and methodically folded his beach chair, tucked the day's newspaper in it, and placed his red and white rolled-up umbrella on top of his right shoulder. "Follow me, gentlemen," Mr. K replied. "This is truly one of the finest days of my life on Esperanza Street."

As the sun's rays cast long shadows on Esperanza Street, most of the families were outside their houses watering or simply admiring their new flower boxes. Some people were cleaning up their little front yards, sweeping the sidewalks, doing a little painting, or picking up the few pieces of trash that remained on the street. As Mr. Kerriokas led the procession, the neighbors stopped what they were doing and shouted a greeting and then clapped and whistled. It was indeed a very small parade but it received a lot of love.

It took the boys a few minutes to install Mr. K's flower box. Removing

the ladders, all three stepped back to see if it was centered properly.

"Thank you, Anthony," Mr. Kerriokas began, "for giving an old man a wonderful present, something to look forward to each day." He paused to take out his white handkerchief and wiped away the tear that trickled down his cheek. "The window box you both made for me is terrific and will bring me a great deal of pleasure, but your greatest gift is that you have made me feel needed and capable of making a contribution. I thought those feelings were gone forever. You have made a lot of people happy, especially me."

Anthony and David didn't know what to say. They gave Mr. K a big hug, looked him in the eyes and shook his hand. "Mr. K," Anthony said, "we wouldn't have a garden if it weren't for you. You will always be my 'Filakas' and friend. Thank you for everything." Anthony grinned and continued, "And, Mr. K, don't forget to water your geraniums. You are the best gardener on Esperanza Street. Everyone will be watching your flowers. David and I are betting yours will be the best." With a wave of their hands, and a "See you tomorrow," the boys headed home.

Chapter

As the end of the summer approached, Anthony's garden continued to grow lovelier each day. Flowers bloomed and passed; new plants took their place, budded, and then they too blossomed. Good as their word, the neighbors of Esperanza Street conscientiously tended their flower boxes, and large red geraniums could be seen from one end of the street to the other.

Anthony and David had just finished their morning weeding and watering and were about to rewind the hose when Mr. Kerriokas pointed out two motorcycle policemen leading a long black limo up the street. It was followed by a police car and four other vehicles.

"I wonder where they are going?" Anthony said out loud.

David shrugged, "Who knows? Mmm, they seem to be slowing down. Hope it's not against the law to raise flowers in the city, Anthony," and he laughed. "We may be in big trouble."

The motorcycle officers passed and then stopped. Then the limo and other cars pulled up to the curb and stopped right in front of Anthony's garden. Uniformed police officers opened the car doors of the limo and the Mayor of the City stepped out, followed by Mr.Cocozza and Anthony's father.

The Mayor strode directly toward Anthony, David and Mr. Kerriokas. Reporters and photographers ran from the other cars to catch up with the Mayor. Neighbors left their houses to see what the commotion was about and to join the fast growing crowd. Anthony's mother and his brother opened the front door and stood on the porch looking down as people ran toward their house. "What was going on?" everyone asked.

A gentleman passed Anthony and began to set up a portable microphone on the porch. Seconds later the Mayor reached Anthony, David and Mr. Kerriokas. He introduced himself and shook hands with each one. He then asked them to join him on Anthony's front steps beside the garden.

Anthony's head was spinning and he could barely manage a "Nice to meet you, Mr. Mayor." He looked questioningly at his father who now stood proudly by his mother on the steps above him. The police had organized the throng into a semi-circle facing Anthony's house. The Mayor picked up the microphone. Spotting Anthony's mother he asked her to come down with her husband to join them.

"Ladies and Gentlemen," the Mayor began, "I have a very special honor to perform today. I want to recognize several outstanding citizens of our city. We are proud to have people like these who live on Esperanza Street. Recently, I learned of two young men and a senior citizen who created this beautiful garden beside me, and generously shared their good fortune with everyone on Esperanza Street." The Mayor turned and looked directly at Anthony, David and Mr. Kerriokas. "Speaking for your government," the Mayor continued," we are very proud of what you have accomplished. On behalf of the city, I would like to present to you these Community Service medallions."

As the Mayor placed the medals around the necks of the boys and Mr. Kerriokas, the crowd cheered and the Mayor returned to the microphone. "Anthony, our country needs young men like you and David who want to improve our cities and to make them healthier and more beautiful places to live. We would like you, David, and your teacher Mr. Cocozza, to represent our city at the 4-H Exhibition and Country Fair. Inside this envelope is a check which should cover all your expenses, and I believe there should be enough extra to pay for seeds and plants for your garden next year. We wish you good luck with your flowers and the 'Mt. Olympus squash'," and then the Mayor winked. "Have a wonderful time."

Anthony's mouth opened but no words came out. He was truly speechless. He turned and looked at David and Mr. Cocozza, who had gigantic grins spread across their faces. Finally it sunk in: he wasn't having another dream. This was real. "Country Fair, here we come," he thought.

The Mayor turned and once more shook hands with everyone. Anthony, now a little more relaxed, looked up at the Mayor and even forgot the microphone was still on. "Thank you, very much, Mr. Mayor. Please wait just a moment." Anthony jumped into his garden and quickly picked a lovely bouquet of flowers. "For your wife, Sir," and he handed them to the Mayor. "Tell her they are from all the people who live on Esperanza Street."

The Mayor took the flowers and thanked the huge crowd that had even grown bigger. "Anthony, I think you know how to treat people as well as flowers. Maybe some day you should think of a career in politics, too." The Mayor smiled and waved as he returned to his car. A few moments later the entourage disappeared down the street.

Anthony, David, and Mr. Cocozza did have a wonderful time at the 4-H Exhibition and Country Fair. Anthony entered several bouquets of flowers and Mr. K's squash in the competitions. They met many other young people from all over the country who had raised flowers, vegetables, and animals. On the final day prizes were awarded, and Anthony was presented with a third place ribbon for his flowers, and Mr. K's squash took second place in the vegetable competition.

When Mr. Cocozza and the boys returned to the city, Anthony presented Mr. Kerriokas with his red ribbon. Mr. Kerriokas couldn't have been prouder. He immediately hung the ribbon on the wall next to pictures of his family and the medallion from the Mayor.

After a handshake, hug and wave, Anthony left Mr. Kerriokas smiling in his doorway. The sun was setting and a long shadow followed Anthony as he slowly walked toward his home. He began thinking of all the people who had helped him over the past six months: Mr. Cocozza and Mr. K,

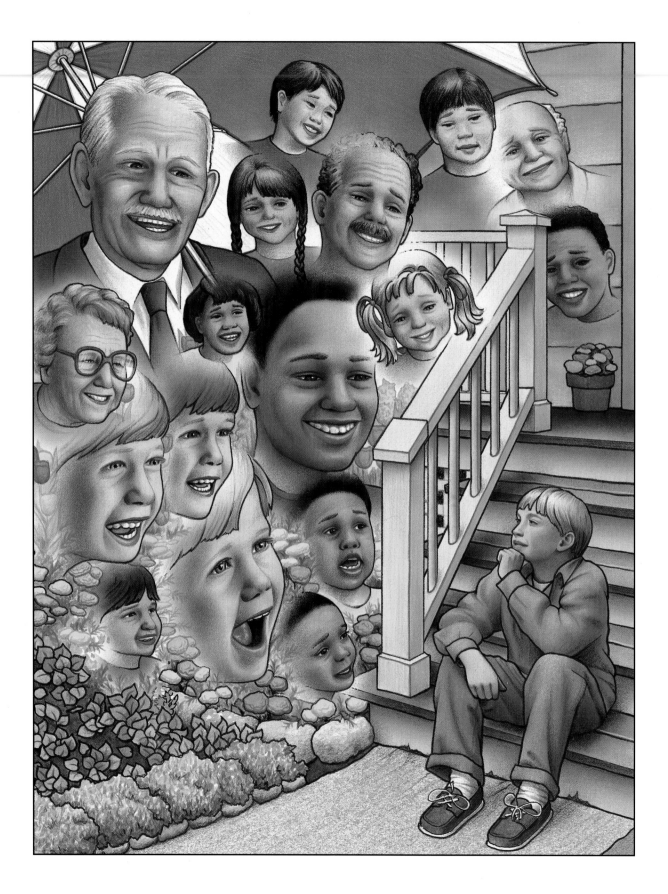

of course, and his good friend David, David's family, and oh, so many neighbors. The little garden, it seemed, had touched everyone on the street.

Anthony paused at his front steps and slowly looked over the garden. Most of the flowers were gone. Brown leaves and withering stalks remained, yet a few hardy gold and yellow marigolds continued to blossom. Anthony raised his head, looking down the street at all the houses which, in one way or another, had changed for the better. Then his gaze focused on the garden. It wasn't hard for him to imagine Mr. Kerriokas with his umbrella surrounded by Anthony's friends and neighbors. They were all smiling at him. Anthony spoke aloud to no one and everyone. "Yes, this is our garden, and maybe next year we'll win a blue ribbon or grow the world's largest squash." Anthony smiled and, laughing at himself, climbed his front steps. In his heart he knew, on Esperanza Streets the world over, dreams can come true.

The End